The Wishing Tree

By Meika Hashimoto · Illustrated by Xindi Yan

HARPER
An Imprint of HarperCollinsPublishers

For every child who knows what
magic feels like.—M.H.

To Steven, for every day with you is
filled with joy and harmony.—X.Y.

The Wishing Tree • Copyright © 2021 by HarperCollins Publishers • All rights reserved
Manufactured in China • No part of this book may be used or reproduced in any manner whatsoever
without written permission except in the case of brief quotations embodied in critical articles and reviews.
For information address HarperCollins Children's Books, a division of HarperCollins Publishers, 195
Broadway, New York, NY 10007. • www.harpercollinschildrens.com
Library of Congress Control Number: 2020947250 • ISBN 978-0-06-274716-7 • The artist used Photoshop to
create the digital illustrations for this book. • Typography by Honee Jang and Caitlin Stamper
21 22 23 24 25 LEO 10 9 8 7 6 5 4 3 2 1 ❖ First Edition

One frosty winter's night, a boy named Theo gazed out his window. He was searching for twinkling lights or merry carolers—anything to remind him that Christmas was only three days away.

But below him, it was dark and quiet. There was no sign of Christmas—not even a single holly.

Theo looked at his letter to Santa. Thinking, he crumpled up the letter, took out a fresh sheet of paper, and sat down.

Instead of a list of toys, Theo wrote down just one wish.

Theo signed the letter, climbed into bed, and drifted off to sleep. While he dreamed, the clock struck midnight. A gust of wind blew through the room and swept his letter out the window.

Borne by a wild winter wind,
the letter tumbled through the air,
across frozen seas

and stormy deserts,

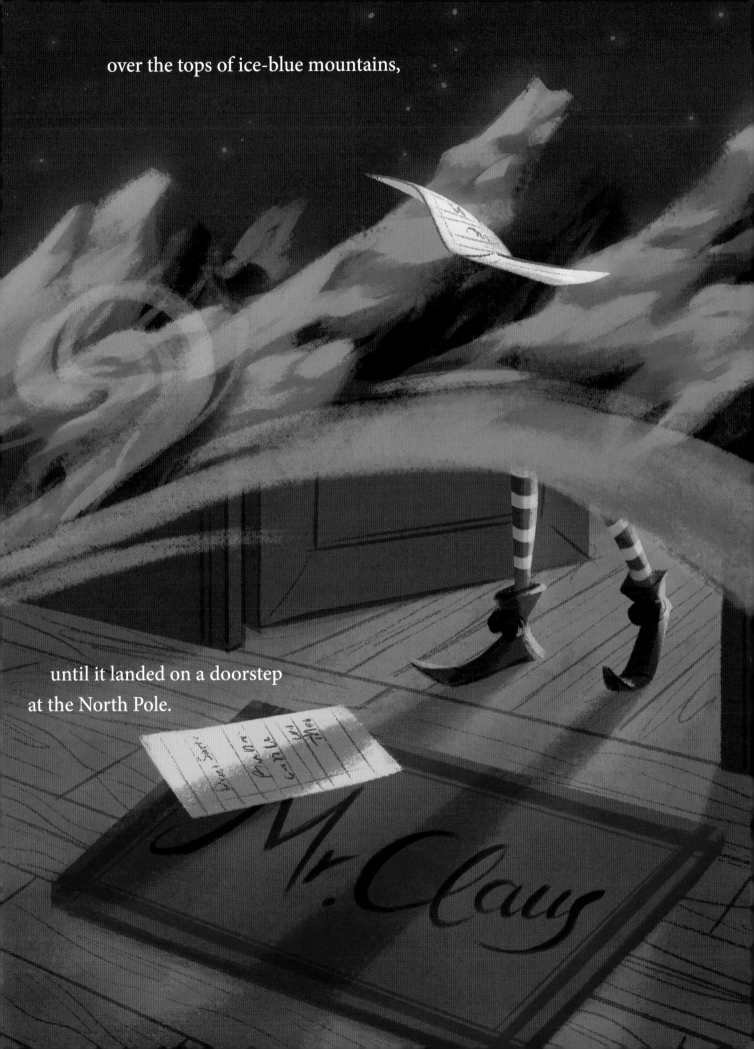

over the tops of ice-blue mountains,

until it landed on a doorstep
at the North Pole.

The next morning, Theo woke to a world covered in snow.
He put on his coat, jumped into his boots, and rushed outside.

After he found his red wooden sled, Theo set off
into the woods, excited to play in the fresh snow.

Swoosh! He sledded down the hill.

Before he knew it, Theo came to a stop in front of a
great pine. Its branches stretched up into the sky, with
needles so bright they seemed to glow. "Property of the
North Pole" was carved into its trunk.

A playful breeze rustled through the tree and a letter floated down.

"Bring joy," Theo read. He peered around the thick tree trunk, certain the letter had come from someone nearby. But no one was there.

Theo shrugged, tucked the letter in his
pocket, and headed home for hot cocoa.

At home, he helped his parents and grandma decorate
the fireplace—their little Christmas tradition.
And then, he had an idea.

Theo ran and dug up a great big box filled with golden
lights and shiny ornaments. He loaded it onto his sled.
"Be right back, Mom!" Theo shouted as he rushed out.

As Theo strolled through the neighborhood, he draped Christmas
lights from the trees and hung ornaments from the bushes.

Night fell, and the streets came to life. And for the first time in a long while, people slowed down to see how pretty their town could be.

The next day, Theo somehow found himself by the great pine again.

Miraculously, as with the first, a letter drifted down. "Find harmony," it read.

This time, Theo knew just what to do.

That evening, Theo walked to his neighbor's house and knocked. When the door opened, he began to sing, quietly at first.

Deck the hall with boughs of holly,
Fa, la, la, la, la, la, la, la, la!

His neighbor paused . . . then she joined in.

At the next house,
they sang "Jingle Bells."

And then it was
"Winter Wonderland."

By the time Theo got to the last house, all of his neighbors had come together in song. Their voices rose, rich and full of joy.

The next morning it was finally Christmas! His grandma made her famous Christmas breakfast. Theo couldn't wait to open his presents. Just as he was about to peek inside his stocking, his parents told him they had to go to work. They promised to be back in time for dinner.

Suddenly, Theo's Christmas lights seemed to dim.

His grandma knew it wasn't the lights, the singing, or even
the gifts that made Christmas special. It was really about
spending it with the people you loved.

So she got an idea. Theo had already brightened the town so much—
maybe there was a way for the town to thank him. She picked up her
phone and invited the townsfolk over for Christmas dinner.

The news of the invitation spread quickly.
Everyone was excited to come together and help
bring the Christmas cheer back to Theo.

That night, neighbor after neighbor bustled into Theo's house carrying platters filled with delicious food. Theo couldn't believe his eyes—and neither could his parents! The whole town was there!

After a hearty feast with jolly good company, Theo's mom asked Grandma and Theo, "Where did you get your ideas?"

"From Theo!" his grandma said.

"Follow me," Theo said with a grin.

Theo led the town to the great pine. As people gathered around, the glowing tree filled the dark woods with soft, magical light.

A small piece of paper drifted into Theo's hands. "This is the letter I wrote to Santa!" he cried. He read it aloud to everyone. "Dear Santa, please show how special Christmas really can be."

Thanks to Theo and the wishing tree, his Christmas wish came true. Everyone could see the magic of Christmas everywhere. The townsfolk began to put their own Christmas wishes on the wishing tree.

Theo couldn't wait until the next year when he could continue
this new holiday tradition of hanging his Christmas wish on
the wishing tree with his family.